Petite Scribe

ISBN:
9 781667 102405

10 9 8 7 6 5 4 3 2 1

JOURNEY JOY

Tale of a Service Dog and Her School Friends

<u>Dedication</u>

To my beautiful daughter Bridget and her husband Justin, whose dedication to the education of children at an early age, has inspired me each day to bring my stories to life. Your kind hearts and spirits have carried me through many tough times. Thank you for always being there for me.

To my granddaughters, Alyssa, Faith, and Ryann who have encouraged and supported me along the way. Thank you for teaching me that inside every child lies the mind of a dreamer. You are so beautiful and I know you will share your kindness, talents, and beauty with the world. I will forever cherish our memories together.

Special recognition goes to Journey Joy, the service dog whose tender heart for children and animals was my motivation for writing this book. If she could talk, I'm sure she would have many fun stories to tell.

My name is Journey Joy,
And I go to school each day.
There are children, babies,
and animals
that I play with along the way.

Hi, Cole, how are you?
I'm happy to see you today.
Please grab the vest upon my back
and we will be on our way!

I will walk you to your class,
each and every day,
making sure you don't get scared,
or get lost along the way.

I'm a service dog, I'll keep you safe,
as I have been trained to do.
While you're playing and having fun,
I'll keep a watchful eye on you.

I love it when you hug my neck!
My tail wags side to side.
It shows me just how much you care,
and fills me up with pride.

Now let's go outside to play,
and meet my animal friends.
You see, they also need my help
when they are out of their pens.

There's my friend Kiki,
the chicken that squawks out loud.
She runs about with excitement
when the kids all gather about.

Over there are my goat friends
that keep me on alert.
Running and jumping around the
school,
and rolling around in the dirt.

Their names are Maisy, Maui, and
Millie,
and don't forget Malani and Moo.
The goats that seem to eat everything,
and sometimes even a shoe!

Then there are some children
that chase the goats around.
No wonder why the goats are jumping
as high up as the clouds.

Now I see Mushu and Mia,
the piglets who follow me around.
They do make such a cute little pair,
making that snorting sound.

And where are those Bunnies,
Winter and Honey, too?
They seem to be hiding somewhere,
as bunnies often do.

I love our birds of many colors.
They watch over us each day.
In the cage they call their home,
not wanting to fly away.

I can see those waddling ducks,
known as Peanut and Butter.
They like to walk around the school,
but mostly stay near the water.

Every day is different,
and there's so much here to see.
But I love my school friends
because they're like my family.

It sometimes feels like a jungle,
with my friends all carefree.
But then again at the end of the day,
there's no place I'd rather be!

About The Author

About The Author

I live in Sun City, Az. When I'm not writing, I am cooking. I love bringing my friends and family together through food. It's such a fun time.

I have a son, and a daughter and three gorgeous granddaughters. I could not be more proud of all of them and their accomplishments.

I live in the desert, so I get to see many different kinds of wildlife. I have quail, rabbits, hawks, and on occasion, a jack rabbit who makes himself at home by digging holes in my yard. How inspiring to write about real life experiences and to share these with children! I am young at heart, so I relate to them and their young minds. They can teach us so much, if we just listen.

Acknowledgements

Thanks to Journey School of Peoria for the amazing job in creating young Kings and Princesses by providing a curriculum where children can learn, explore, and investigate their world in a nature- based environment.

Many thanks to Elizabeth Eichelberger, the greatest illustrator I could ever imagine. Her artistic talents superseded my expectations. Thanks again for your patience.

A very special thanks to my dear friend and Author, Penny Estelle. You always encouraged me to put my words on paper and I can't thank you enough for pushing me forward. Your "Good Buddy" forever.

To my sisters, Linda and Sharon, you may live miles away, but are always near to my heart. You are my best advocates and I love you dearly.

For my son, Blake; though you may be far away, you are always on my mind. I love you and be safe.

About The Illustrator

Elizabeth Eichelberger fell in love with art at a very early age. She cannot remember a single day where she did not at least doodle something.

Presently (as of August 2021), Elizabeth Eichelberger has her original cover art and or full illustrations published in a combined total of 20 books, as well as being the creator of several logos. From Digital art to oil paintings, and from formatting books to creating book trailers, Elizabeth has dove in head first and loves her artistic universe! Whether it be creating clay sculptures or 3D virtual reality sculptures, chances are, if Elizabeth is not illustrating, she can be found working on some sort of art. For more on Elizabeth, scan QR code or visit ALYSATHENA.COM

CPSIA information can be obtained
at www.ICGtesting.com
Printed in the USA
BVHW011709050921
615986BV00021B/806